mini saga
competition 200
for Primary Schools from Young Writers in associat

Tiny Tales

Southern Fiction

First published in Great Britain in 2007 by
Young Writers, Remus House, Coltsfoot Drive,
Peterborough, PE2 9JX
Tel (01733) 890066 Fax (01733) 313524
All Rights Reserved

© Copyright Contributors 2007
SB ISBN 978-1-84431-359-4

Disclaimer
Young Writers has maintained every effort
to publish stories that will not cause offence.
Any stories, events or activities relating to individuals
should be read as fictional pieces and not construed
as real-life character portrayal.

Foreword

Young Writers was established in 1991, with the aim of encouraging the children and young adults of today to think and write creatively. Our latest primary school competition, *Tiny Tales*, posed an exciting challenge for these young authors: to write, in no more than fifty words, a story encompassing a beginning, a middle and an end. We call this the mini saga.

Tiny Tales Southern Fiction is our latest offering from the wealth of young talent that has mastered this incredibly challenging form. With such an abundance of imagination, humour and ability evident in such a wide variety of stories, these young writers cannot fail to enthral and excite with every tale.

Contents

All Saints Junior School, Hastings
Aimee Gibbs (10) 13
Steven Edmett (10) 14
Joshua Dowler (10) 15
Albie Adams (10) 16
Coral Winterburn (10) 17
Jack Froude (10) 18
Frank Sherwood (10) 19
Pollyanna Groves (10) 20
Lewis Todd (10) 21
Jake Brett (10) 22
Zachary Dunning (9) 23
Ryan Boakes (10) 24
Ashleigh Haynes (10) 25
Harrison Cox (11) 26
Joshua Heap (11) 27
Cameron White (11) 28
Tanisha Charman (11) 29
Rhys Climpson (11) 30
Pollyanna Riggs (11) 31
Alexandra Peckham (11) 32
Pasha Milburn (11) 33
Grace Cudmore (11) 34
Jessamy Dunning (11) 35
Tom Wisden (11) 36
Rosie Jeakings (11) 37
Rebecca Andrews (11) 38
Luke Barbary (11) 39
Bethany Burgess (10) 40
Elisha Winchester (10) 41
Rowan Geering (10) 42
Christopher Cook (10) 43
Jake Couchman (9) 44
Tom Borthwick (9) 45
George Peters (10) 46
Alfie Bowenmith (10) 47
Sam Jarvis (10) 48
Florence Graham (10) 49
Molly Hugh (11) 50
Chloe Brock-Everitt (11) 51
Jessica Bartlett (11) 52
Oliver de la Harpe (11) 53
Natasha Dockerill (11) 54
Carla Flack (10) 55
India Mallindine (11) 56

Chacombe CE Primary School, Chacombe
Daisy Byrne (11) 57
Deanna Bayford (10) 58
Kieran Flint (10) 59
Raahat Kaduji (11) 60

Roberta Byrne (10) 61
Charlie Milne (10) 62
Ellie McClements (10) 63
Bronnen Manning (11) 64
Andrew Newstead (11)................................65
Katie Smart (11) 66
Naomi Hay (10) 67

Cumnor CE Primary School, Cumnor

Anna Murphy (10)..68
Lydia Carter (10)..69
Amelia Gilio (10) 70
Zelie Hudson (9)..71
Cole Thornicroft (10) 72
Mark Briggs (10)..73
Fraser Shields (10) 74
Olivia Gardner (10) 75
Steven Dent (10) 76
Lydie Thorn (10) 77
Timmy Middleton (10) 78
Brannon Nicholls (10)....................................79
Amy Livesey (10) 80
Chantal Olavesen (10) 81
Tim Spencer Tanfield (10) 82

Datchet St Mary's CE Primary School, Datchet

Sian O'Shea (11) 83
Emily Perry (10) 84

Edward Feild CP Primary School, Kidlington

David Rees (11)...85
Callum McGuire (11) 86
Jasmin Sims (7)...87
Tomos Hooper (11) 88
Lucy Truman (10) 89
Alison Brodie (11)..90
Julia Brain (11) 91
Joe Howes (11) 92
Jack Sims (10)...93
Bethany Hutson (11) 94
Genevieve Tomes (9)....................................95
Ellishia Chard (9) 96
Abigail Teasdale (8).......................................97
Charlie Nutt (11) 98
Connor Micallef (11) 99
Zoe Hart (11) 100
Holly Lyford (11) 101
Maisie Siret (11) 102
Matthew Cunningham (8)...........................103
Skye Turner (10) 104
Kamran Afzal (10)..105
Kieran Kilcoyne (8) 106
Toby Cole (9) 107
Natasha Owen (9) 108
Chloe Pearce-Higgins (9)...........................109
Georgia Allen (9) 110
Alex Hedges (11)...111
Melissa Fry (9 112
Scarlett Tomes (11) 113

Emma Gough (7) 114

First Tower School, St Helier
Katie Le Masurier (10) 115
Francesca Monticelli (10) 116
Chloe Dashwood (10) 117
Nathan Samson (10) 118
Isabella De Freitas (10) 119
Jamie Hamilton (10) 120
Calum Fowler (10) 121
Rosie Lee (10) 122
Cole Courval (10) 123
Jonathan Williams (10) 124
Lucy Fraser (10) 125

Hambrough Primary School, Southall
Gaganpreet Bangar (9) 126
Safiya Ali (10) 127
Divya Thankaraj (10) 128
Alisha Janjua (10) 129
Zionita Rathod (10) 130
Shivani Ohari (9) 131
Naurane Asif (8) 132
Hamza Butt (8) 133
Shabana Mussa (7) 134
Fatima Ali (8) 135
Jigar Santilal 136
Ramanjit Marway (9) 137
Rajan Mann (9) 138
Preetam Virdee (9) 139
Sarika Chauhan (9) 140

Ruth Ladani (8) 141
Rajinder Chana (8) 142
Marya Razzaq (9) 143

Kintbury St Mary's CE Primary School, Kintbury
Sam Robins (10) 144
Julia Thorp (10) 145
Toby Chandler (10) 146
Louise Fell (10) 147
Jack Moore (10) 148
Benjamin Grey (10) 149
Saskia Marshall (10) 150
Sinead Graham (10) 151
Amy Sidhu (10) 152
Kieren Phipps (11) 153
Chloe Boulter (11) 154
Sky Caves (9) 155

Lady Eleanor Holles Junior School, Hampton Hill
Gee-Heon Kim (11) 156
Lucinda Smith (11) 157
Maria Griston (11) 158
Nicole Quah (11) 159
Emily Smith (10) 160
Rosamund Downer (10) 161
Imogen Thwaites (11) 162
Monica Gupta (11) 163
Kirsten Chaplin (11) 164
Ellie Roberts (11) 165

Anna Stuart (11) 166

Littledown School, Slough
Joshua Daulton (11) 167

Loddon Primary School, Earley
Pratham Mishra (9) 168
Urvi Bihani (9) 169
Mouadjul Miah (8) 170
Sophie Busby (9) 171
Hannah Pollard (9) 172
Esther Bilton (10) 173
Ishwari Sharma (10) 174
Megan Cadman (10) 175
Emma Billington (10) 176
Leah Martins (10) 177
Chloe Beckett (10) 178

St John's RC Primary School, Banbury
Benjamin Mitchelmore (8) 179
Joe Mates (7) 180
Eleanor Claridge (8) 181
Matthew Cummings-Coules (8) 182

St Mary's Catholic Primary School, Maidenhead
Tom Mulcahy (10) 183
Zack Minter (10) 184
Victoria Paul (11) 185
Jack Cooper (11) 186
Elisa Di-Rosa (11) 187
Shannon Jarnak (11) 188

Oscar Rutishauser-Mills (11) 189
Bryony Mulholland (11) 190
Luis Homer (11) 191
Ryan Manuel (11) 192
Max Barnes (11) 193
Isabelle Smith (11) 194
Megan McCaffrey (11) 195
Israr Akhtar (11) 196
Katie Greet (11) 197
Mateusz Wzietal (11) 198
Isabella Williams (11) 199
Callum Edwards (11) 200
James Herron (10) 201
Robert Nash (11) 202
Juno Tejeda (11) 203

Stoke Row CE Primary School, Henley-on-Thames
Kayleigh Ramsay (9) 204
Mary Lobo (8) 205

The Batt CE School, Witney
Kieran Tang (11) 206
Kirby Henderson-Sowerby (11) 207
Connie Manning (11) 208
Charlotte Roberts (11) 209
Christopher Macdonald (10) 210
Ash Myall (10) 211
Joslyn Beadle (10) 212
Taylor Lee (10) 213
Bethany Knight (10) 214

Lydia Locke (10)	215
Edward Longden (10)	216
Ysabela Torres (10)	217
William Keating (10)	218
Harry Hamblin (9)	219
Michael Phelps (10)	220
Carenza Glithero (10)	221
Georgina Holliday (10)	222
Lucy Nobes (10)	223
Rosie Meredith (10)	224
Fraser Stokes (10)	225
Holly Warne (10)	226
Marcus Camm (10)	227
Jessica Berry (9)	228

Uplands Primary School, Sandhurst

Eli Mohammed (9)	229
Ria Wingfield (9)	230
Emma Chiles (9)	231
James Purser (9)	232
Katie McCann (9)	233
Jarrad Fry (9)	234
Callum Sanders (9)	235
Krista Lalli (9)	236
Adeela Bhutta (9)	237
Jodie Hughes (9)	238
Lexy Ward (8)	239
Alex Davies (9)	240
Phoebe Coleman (8)	241
Jasmine Husband (9)	242
Natasha Hunt (9)	243
Zoe Weir (9)	244
Alfie Gibbons (9)	245
Yasmin Joseph (8)	246
Abby Williams (7)	247

Whitelands Park Primary School, Thatcham

Sharmin Khan (10)	248
Katie Turner (10)	249
Matthew Jackson (10)	250
Luke Stevens (9)	251
Holly Hobson (10)	252
Kieran McClair (10)	253
James Salter (10)	254
Amy Tucker (9)	255
Siobhan O'Brien (10)	256
Joshua Glanville (10)	257
Georgia Moss (10)	258
Alexander McLean-Barr (9)	259
Craig Macmillan (10)	260
Hannah Russell (10)	261
Mark Lavender (10)	262
Charlotte Kavanagh (10)	263
Bradd Clay (10)	264
Annie Lawrence (10)	265
Roee Steinberg (9)	266
Joseph Robson (10)	267
David Lovelock (10)	268

The Mini Sagas

Tiny Tales Southern Fiction

Who Goes There?

I lay there, was I dead? Where was my gun? Where was the enemy? I tried to move, I was tied down! Suddenly, I heard a voice, 'Ner, ner.' What was that?
'Boo, got you!'
There it was again, I looked, it was … Mickey! I hate playing cowboys with him.

Aimee Gibbs (10)
All Saints Junior School, Hastings

A Holiday Of A Lifetime

Slovakian ice caves were said to have yeti ice trolls lurking in the shadows. We had reached 10,000 feet below ground level. We were in the bowels of the Earth, I turned the icy corner and I was face to face with … yeti! I sprinted, there was no escape!

Steven Edmett (10)
All Saints Junior School, Hastings

Untitled

I was at the book area when the electric went off. There was a bizarre thing, there were glowing potions. I mixed the red potion with the yellow potion gently; I was extremely frightened about it. The electric went on, I was only scared of a drink, it was bizarre.

Joshua Dowler (10)
All Saints Junior School, Hastings

The Aeroplane

My hair stood up on my back as the wheel started to move. It went even faster and at that point we took off, it was flying! We were going higher, higher and then we were so high that we could fly. I asked my mum, 'Are we there yet?'

Albie Adams (10)
All Saints Junior School, Hastings

Tiny Tales Southern Fiction

Untitled

I pushed open the door and there standing in front of me was the ugliest great beast, it was my teacher! She gave me homework! I screamed before I woke up. It was a dream, thank goodness. But I had homework in my hand? I was scared and shaken!

Coral Winterburn (10)
All Saints Junior School, Hastings

Super Dad

I crept up to the door and knocked hard. The sound echoed through the castle. Suddenly I heard someone whisper, 'Billy, Billy!' I froze, someone was running up to the door. I saw … 'Billy get up!' It was Dad. He had rescued me from the big, hairy, angry monkey.

Jack Froude (10)
All Saints Junior School, Hastings

A Load Of Nonsense

One day, on the planet Cribet, a man was counting his biscuits on the beach. For those of you who don't know, biscuits are money there. Suddenly a robotic spaceman appeared in front of him and said, 'I want planet Mars.' So the man gave him a Mars bar.

Frank Sherwood (10)
All Saints Junior School, Hastings

Bath Time

'Come on dear, have you finished your dinner?' shouted Mum.
'OK, I'm going!' sadly whispered Tommy.
'Don't be long,' exclaimed Mum.
Two hours later ... 'Are you wrinkly yet?' asked Mum.
'I'm drowning, help, help!' Tommy shouted.
'Get out of the bath now!' said Mum.
'No really, help, help!' shouted Tommy.

Pollyanna Groves (10)
All Saints Junior School, Hastings

The Monster

The creature came closer and closer, I became more and more scared of what might happen next. It roared, 'I'm coming!'
In an attempt to lose him I jolted to the left, my attempt was in vain. I was so scared. Was this it, the end?
'Tag, you are it!'

Lewis Todd (10)
All Saints Junior School, Hastings

The Darkness

Badly shaken, I was terrified. I almost fainted; I could hear my colleagues being defeated. The creaking was getting closer. The pressure was building up! I could hear the door open, then there was silence. Although I was hidden he found me.

'40–40 home, I found Jake, I win!'

Jake Brett (10)
All Saints Junior School, Hastings

The Thing

I arrived home from school; it was quiet, too quiet. Suddenly a shadow emerged and so did a floorboard creak; the shadow became larger and larger. A black figure appeared, it got closer and closer. It stopped. I froze. It opened its mouth, 'Zac, time to do your homework now!'

Zachary Dunning (9)
All Saints Junior School, Hastings

Terror In The Field

Apprehensively I walked home at midnight through the deserted field. My heart raced rapidly. Roars of death were carried through. Suddenly a creature came from the distance, as it scurried towards me I ran for my life away from the roads screaming unbelievably! Approaching … louder … closer … 'Want a lift?' 'Sure!'

Ryan Boakes (10)
All Saints Junior School, Hastings

A Spell

I was about to read to my dad when he fell right into a really deep sleep, I whispered to myself, 'I will do a spell!' Suddenly my dad's eyes flickered and he woke up as I was waving my wand! He caught me in the act, I was surprised!

Ashleigh Haynes (10)
All Saints Junior School, Hastings

Destruction Of The World

It was early morning, sun was rising, the sun was much hotter and closer. I turned on the telly, all there was on was the news saying 'It's time to die. The Big Bang is coming!' About thirty minutes later the Earth cracked in half, everyone died painfully!

Harrison Cox (11)
All Saints Junior School, Hastings

Untitled

As I fall off a cliff, my throat tightens, I feel tingling in my bones as my foot slips down and down … I hit the floor unconscious.

Joshua Heap (11)
All Saints Junior School, Hastings

The Scary Journey

It was a dark, gloomy night. Then I heard a strange moving in the bushes and there was my cousin Sam. His face was covered in blood and then I took him, got him cleaned up and we both played football together.

Cameron White (11)
All Saints Junior School, Hastings

Tiny Tales Southern Fiction

My Surprise Birthday

The day began with a big surprise when I woke up because my bed was covered in confetti. I looked under my bed, there were lots of presents. I wondered, *I know it's my birthday but where is everybody?* I went downstairs, everybody jumped out at me, wow, cool!

Tanisha Charman (11)
All Saints Junior School, Hastings

What Happened To Hitler?

I was standing over a small fire cooking dinner when the bomb exploded. Everyone filed out of their houses and I saw Hitler. He was a small man with a strange moustache. Hitler raised his gun and fired in my direction. What happened to Hitler? I didn't live to see.

Rhys Climpson (11)
All Saints Junior School, Hastings

Falling

I am falling again and again, climbing up and throwing myself off. I wake up drenched in cold sweat. It happens every night since my mum fell off the building. Was she pushed? I don't know, I'm just falling …

Pollyanna Riggs (11)
All Saints Junior School, Hastings

Alien Invasion

It was a clear night. Everyone in the village was asleep. Suddenly there was a bright green glow from the sky. A huge oval orb appeared and landed in a nearby field. A hole appeared and everyone in town woke and checked the window. They gasped, they had landed!

Alexandra Peckham (11)
All Saints Junior School, Hastings

The Yeti

I stood up to my knees in snow. The wind howled and my hands were numb. Through the swirling snow I saw a figure. I gasped what breath was still inside me … a yeti! The yeti roared.
'Cut! The girl's in the way!'
Phew! It's just a film!

Pasha Milburn (11)
All Saints Junior School, Hastings

Science Lab Terror

I ended up in a science lab. What was going to happen to me? A mad scientist came over and said to me, 'You will die!'
I screamed because of the 'Game over' sign on my computer game.

Grace Cudmore (11)
All Saints Junior School, Hastings

Birthday Hell

It was like any normal day, I walked home from school I asked my mum and dad, 'What's up?' They didn't answer but smiled carrying a large knife. 'Help!' I screamed but to my surprise they cut a slice of cake.
'Happy birthday Jess!'

Jessamy Dunning (11)
All Saints Junior School, Hastings

Football Disaster

I was walking in the beautiful park! I was playing footie with my mate Eddie. We were just having a kick about, booting the ball really high and then suddenly it dropped into the waters. I dived in after it but I remembered I could not swim, oh no!

Tom Wisden (11)
All Saints Junior School, Hastings

The Trip

The car began to rattle along the road. I thought about the dark matter in hand, my hands and feet were trembling. I felt terrified. Mum parked up, she said, 'Don't worry.'
That was easy for her to say. Many people had been here before; I walked into the dentist.

Rosie Jeakings (11)
All Saints Junior School, Hastings

The Day My Mum Stopped Loving Me

It was around five in the morning when my mum entered my room, I wondered what my mum was doing so I looked up to see my mum stuffing all my clothes in a suitcase. Suddenly I awoke in deep, deep shock, but not in my bed, where was I?

Rebecca Andrews (11)
All Saints Junior School, Hastings

Untitled

Sweat was pouring down the back of my neck; looking down from a building I was pushed! I'm still falling … never stopping … always falling.

Luke Barbary (11)
All Saints Junior School, Hastings

The Figure

Nervously Stephanie picked at the rusty lock of the chamber as the lightning flashed. *Bang!* The door flew open, the silence was broken. A face peered from the dark void, it was horrid! His distorted body melted as she tried to distinguish its features. *Argh!* Curiously, was it worth it?

Bethany Burgess (10)
All Saints Junior School, Hastings

Tiny Tales Southern Fiction

Upside-Down Bat

Bolly, the bat, was trying to get to sleep. She lay on the hay, but she still couldn't get to sleep. So she called her doctor, the doctor said he'll be there soon. When the doctor arrived he realised why Bolly couldn't sleep, she needed to hang herself upside down.

Elisha Winchester (10)
All Saints Junior School, Hastings

Untitled

Mel was jumping on a Jelly Bean castle. She was smiling at the girl. She was queen of the world and she was drinking a fruit cocktail. She was wearing a diamond necklace and she was married to King Marco. Will this last forever? But was it a dream?

Rowan Geering (10)
All Saints Junior School, Hastings

Tiny Tales Southern Fiction

The Struggle

He sat there struggling. Bill had forgotten about dinner. He could hear his mum coming up the stairs. Blood was pouring out his mouth but he kept on trying. His mum was on the landing now, suddenly his tooth came free.
'Dinner,' shouted his mum. He was just in time.

Christopher Cook (10)
All Saints Junior School, Hastings

The Flame Man

One dark windy night, Flameman was walking along Cosy Beach. Peering through the darkness, he figures out the shape of Waterman's Waterboat on the horizon. Running back to his cave, he grabbed his bike and sped down to the beach to meet the horizon. *Vroom*, Waterman's Waterboat had gone!

Jake Couchman (9)
All Saints Junior School, Hastings

Tiny Tales Southern Fiction

The Attic Monkey

Once upon a time there was a boy named Tom. He heard a weird sound in the attic. One night Tom quietly went up in to the attic and looked around, there were cobwebs everywhere, it smelt like gone off bread, the monster was his dad unfortunately, unlucky!

Tom Borthwick (9)
All Saints Junior School, Hastings

Star Worms

One summer's evening on the kitchen table Darth Worm stood in front of Luke Wormpocket. 'I am your wormpa Luke,' he shouted. The giant human shoved a pink bowl of hot yellow stuff on the table.
'No,' said Luke as he forcefully pushed his dad into the custard.

George Peters (10)
All Saints Junior School, Hastings

Tiny Tales Southern Fiction

The Book

I was quickly walking in the street then I saw an old man in a dark alley. He was clutching a book, he let me see it. Softly my mum called me back; I'll never forget what I saw!

Alfie Bowenmith (10)
All Saints Junior School, Hastings

The Weird Match

Finally it was Saturday afternoon, I was watching a football match at Old Trafford. The teams were coming out, one team were mice then the second team came out, they were monsters. It was mice Vs monsters. It was a death-threatening match up. The monsters ripped up the stadium.

Sam Jarvis (10)
All Saints Junior School, Hastings

Nightmare

Bang! 'Help!' Squeals of laughter blotted out any human speech, we tried to gag it but it just bit our fingers. I held its legs down but it was no use. Mum was shouting, finally it had ended. 'It's a nightmare getting a nappy on that baby,' Mum told me.

Florence Graham (10)
All Saints Junior School, Hastings

A Spooky Experience

Shivering, she approached the gates, they loomed over her like colossal trees, the vast space beyond was littered with groups of hideous giants, chattering and cackling. Suddenly she glimpsed an immense ogre approaching her.

Towering over her, he opened his fang-loaded jaws, 'Welcome to secondary school,' he whispered kindly.

Molly Hugh (11)
All Saints Junior School, Hastings

Cheeky Milo

Milo absolutely loved lemonade, it was his favourite drink. One day he drank a whole glass of lemonade and he felt the bubbles tickle his belly, go up his nose and he let out a huge great *burp!*
'Milo, what was that?' yelled his mum.
'I'm sorry,' he replied cheekily.

Chloe Brock-Everitt (11)
All Saints Junior School, Hastings

The Metal Object

The dog dived. He floated in a world of apple cores, banana skins, wrappers and food. He sailed the seven seas, juice, water, Coke, lemonade etc. He drifted in and out playing around. A boulder landed on the East Hill, a cookie! This was heaven! Rubbish bins are fun places.

Jessica Bartlett (11)
All Saints Junior School, Hastings

Tiny Tales Southern Fiction

The Future Tale Of Greenland

I was born on an island called Greenland. In the year 2010 I hadn't had a life as such however, in the year 2022 the island of Greenland was flooded. Nobody escaped from this accident so now it shall be a lost city of Greenland, now and for evermore.

Oliver de la Harpe (11)
All Saints Junior School, Hastings

The Beast

It was a dark and gloomy day. The rain thumped down on the windowpane. Suddenly the lights switched off.
There was a bright glow at the end, the beast approached me. I shut my eyes, I felt a brush of wind, I opened my eyes, I saw my teacher!

Natasha Dockerill (11)
All Saints Junior School, Hastings

Tiny Tales Southern Fiction

Boo

I crept up the ladder of my bunk bed. Below, my brother was sleeping soundly. He didn't stir as the bed creaked under my weight. It was the time. He had to be woken, *'Boo!'* I shouted. *'Argh,'* he screamed. It was time for school. 'Don't do that,' he said.

Carla Flack (10)
All Saints Junior School, Hastings

The Beast Baby

Spilt milk for a river, a banana for a boat, potato rocks and boulders and even a cauliflower goat. A giant monster with only two teeth. Swallowed it all whole until … he squashed his boat, put his arm in the river and cried when he choked on some boulders.

India Mallindine (11)
All Saints Junior School, Hastings

The Noisy Night

'Tonight,' I said, 'tonight I *will* stay awake.' At nine o'clock I crept downstairs and put the TV on. Something moved amongst the shadows, *bang!* The kitchen, someone's in the kitchen. The door started opening. I ran out the room, 'Dad!' I cried.
'You should be in bed!' replied Dad.

Daisy Byrne (11)
Chacombe CE Primary School, Chacombe

It

As I walked down the street something rustled in the bushes. I turned around and saw nothing. I heard the noise again, again I saw nothing. I ran home, there was a knock at the door; it was my brother, he said, 'Why did you run away from me?'

Deanna Bayford (10)
Chacombe CE Primary School, Chacombe

A Scary Dream

He lay hidden and in silence. He knew the beast was going to kill him. He did not know what was chasing him, that's why he was still running. *Argh!* He was going to kill me. Suddenly he realised it was a dream, he went back to bed.

Kieran Flint (10)
Chacombe CE Primary School, Chacombe

The Vacant Planet

All of a sudden the ground began to shake. Piercing screams were heard all around as citizens fled from the planet. Air was beginning to run out. Poisonous gasses filled the sky. Moments later the vacant planet began to crumble. Now no longer existing in the silent sombreness of space.

Raahat Kaduji (11)
Chacombe CE Primary School, Chacombe

The Potion That Went Wrong

I stand there pouring the red liquid into the blue. I say, 'Magic potion' five times then pour the red and blue into plain clear liquid. I then pour it into a hat then *bang!* It turns into a rabbit; it was supposed to turn into a dog though!

Roberta Byrne (10)
Chacombe CE Primary School, Chacombe

The Beast

I sat down. I had sweat running down my face. A big beast walked into the room, 'Tom I'm your new head teacher Mrs Tuffball. I'm afraid you're in trouble, Tom!' I wanted to scream. I quickly ran out of the room, teachers surrounded me, I was trapped!

Charlie Milne (10)
Chacombe CE Primary School, Chacombe

Tiny Tales Southern Fiction

The High Dive

I stand there shivering. My legs are wobbling. I take my legs further on the plank. I close my eyes and I fall. *Splash!* That was fun, can I do it again?

Ellie McClements (10)
Chacombe CE Primary School, Chacombe

Jack The Ripper

Jack the Ripper, a mean mysterious man lives in Death Valley. He killed his first victim on the 20th February 1493. Jack was in Death Valley. Suddenly he revealed his razorblades and plunged them into his victim, he slowly pushed his knife into their guts. Their lives faded away.

Bronnen Manning (11)
Chacombe CE Primary School, Chacombe

Mission Possible

Will flew through the Indian skies; he jumped from his plane plummeting to the ground. He activated his parachute and went into the villain's base. Will set a bomb on the wall, he got into the car and then the bomb exploded. Will's mission was successfully complete.

Andrew Newstead (11)
Chacombe CE Primary School, Chacombe

Scared Away

It was dark as a young girl in a witch outfit ran screaming down the path. In the doorway of the house there was a figure dressed up, it was Hallowe'en and he just scared the young trick or treater away.

Katie Smart (11)
Chacombe CE Primary School, Chacombe

The Hunter

One day in a spooky cave, there lying down on the floor was a little girl, shaking around on the ice-cold floor. Suddenly something came closer and closer, you could hear it coming nearer. Then she turned around and it picked her up, she screamed 'It's a huge hunter!'

Naomi Hay (10)
Chacombe CE Primary School, Chacombe

The Tea Party

Walking through a gate I saw three creatures. One hare wearing a tutu, one man dressed as a rapper and a mouse sleeping. *Pop!* Balloon popped. The mouse woke up and then fell asleep. *Pop!* Another balloon popped. *Splat!* This time the mouse fell in the cake, yum-yum!

Anna Murphy (10)
Cumnor CE Primary School, Cumnor

The Jelly Baby, Muffin Man, Gingerbread And The Greedy Boy

Gingerbread Man, Muffin Man and Jelly Baby met greedy boy who said, 'I'm going to eat you.' Jelly Baby made a house out of jelly, Gingerbread Man of gingerbread, Muffin Man of cake. The boy came along ate jelly and cake houses, he was too full to eat gingerbread house.

Lydia Carter (10)
Cumnor CE Primary School, Cumnor

Dangerous Drains

I'm walking, *splash!* I've fallen down the drain. *Wow!* I'm on a ship and there's treasure but *argh!* Rats are scurrying out of it. They're on me now this can't get any worse. It just did – sewage is coming through a pipe and I'm getting washed downstream, *help, help!*

Amelia Gilio (10)
Cumnor CE Primary School, Cumnor

Phone Call From The Dead!

Ring-ring! Sam picked up the phone, 'Hello?'
'Hi, tell the lady going past with the dog happy birthday from Uncle Josh.'
Sam was confused but went out to the lady and said, 'This man wanted to say happy birthday from Uncle Josh.'
'But dear Josh died two months ago!'

Zelie Hudson (9)
Cumnor CE Primary School, Cumnor

The Persuaded Puppy

One day there was a little puppy called Max. He was very lonely and had no one to play with. Then Sally the snake came but she wasn't acting the same, 'Let's go to my place.'
At Sally's place she had gone into the kitchen, then she grabbed his tail …

Cole Thornicroft (10)
Cumnor CE Primary School, Cumnor

The Plane Crash

They were flying into battle, George and Alexander were attacking General Grievous's ship. Suddenly, Alexander had got some bug droids on his a-wing. 'George get them off me,' said Alexander.

'Yes Sir,' George replied. *Bang!* The bug droids were destroyed but Alexander's a-wing was going in circles and then ... *crash!*

Mark Briggs (10)
Cumnor CE Primary School, Cumnor

The Invisible Cheesecake

I was starving for my pudding, badly drooling all over my mouth. Finally I heard a bang on the table, there was an empty plate but I could feel something, it felt like cheesecake but why could my dad see it and I couldn't? *Pop!* The cheesecake appeared, wow!

Fraser Shields (10)
Cumnor CE Primary School, Cumnor

Tiny Tales Southern Fiction

The Runaway

I could hear footsteps behind me, I was scared. It took seconds to glance behind. There they were running towards me, I shouted to the others, 'Run!' With all my strength I picked Lucy up, we ran as fast as we could and then suddenly we ran into a battle.

Olivia Gardner (10)
Cumnor CE Primary School, Cumnor

The Serpent

It was long and stringy and covered in a slimy red substance. Suddenly I was fighting with it. It was whipping my face with its tail and flipping back and forth and back and forth and suddenly it disappeared down a hole! Then I found out I was eating spaghetti.

Steven Dent (10)
Cumnor CE Primary School, Cumnor

Tiny Tales Southern Fiction

When Everything Goes Black

Over the hills of snow I scrambled, looking over my shoulder to check if the thing was still chasing me. I could see its four eyes glinting maliciously. Its toothy grin getting wider, it licked its lips, its mouth opened wide then the screen went blank! I hate powercuts.

Lydie Thorn (10)
Cumnor CE Primary School, Cumnor

Helmsdeep Battle

The sky was dark and gloomy. People were scared. Families hid in caves. The wall vibrated as the sound of the enemy got closer, fear built up inside me. The first strike of my sword was the hardest, we kept telling ourselves we would have victory, faith was with us.

Timmy Middleton (10)
Cumnor CE Primary School, Cumnor

The Hairy Peary Blob

A blob fell from the black tree. It was covered by hairs and pears. It slurped along the road towards the farm. It slipped around the farmhouse and slid towards the pigsty … *scrape!* It was scraped into a pig trough where a huge pig gobbled it completely up.

Brannon Nicholls (10)
Cumnor CE Primary School, Cumnor

My Dream

I was falling through the Earth, everything was destroyed. I looked around and all I could see was darkness, something or someone was calling me. I felt a sharp pain in my arm as my eyes flicked open and my vision became clear, I was in my bedroom again.

Amy Livesey (10)
Cumnor CE Primary School, Cumnor

Tiny Tales Southern Fiction

I Ran!

I ran faster than the wind. I hurtled towards the church. I was sweating, overcome with fright. *Eek!* screeched the door. I stood there, breathless. There it was. I watched it horrified. It turned and spotted me! Petrified, I opened my mouth to scream. It came closer. *Argh!* I ran …

Chantal Olavesen (10)
Cumnor CE Primary School, Cumnor

The Chase

Danny kept on running, he didn't dare stop. He looked behind him, it was still on his tail, the half-man, half-monkey. Danny was becoming more scared by the second. Suddenly Danny lost his foot and tripped and as quick as a flash the monster was on him, *argh!*

Tim Spencer Tanfield (10)
Cumnor CE Primary School, Cumnor

The Potent Portrait

In one captivating moment the portrait seized my absolute essence. I stared intently, scrutinising every detail, it blankly studied me and blinked! I clasped my hands in deep thought, surprisingly the image repeated this. The stark realisation dawned on me … was the portrait of myself or was I the portrait?

Sian O'Shea (11)
Datchet St Mary's CE Primary School, Datchet

The Perilous Journey

I step into the tunnel and shiver. I see a monster, stalking shadows. It's a cat! Run and hide! I dart towards the door and lock it behind me. I have a right to be scared, I'm only a mouse. I just wish the journey to Grandpa's wasn't so scary.

Emily Perry (10)
Datchet St Mary's CE Primary School, Datchet

Tiny Tales Southern Fiction

The Unknown

I was searching, ancient forgotten treasures coming to sight as I dug, clawed and tunnelled my way through mile upon mile of rubbish. Suddenly a glimpse of hope. Digging madly, I pined as my goal came in sight, two, no one more scrape. 'Yes,' I cried, 'my teddy bear!'

David Rees (11)
Edward Feild CP Primary School, Kidlington

My Treacherous Fall

I plummeted to my black grave falling sharply, I screeched, I was terrified. Hitting my gloomy pit I was consumed by loads of tiny crazed objects then a malicious hand yanked me out of my ball pit, it was time to battle with the beast that was … my moronic sister.

Callum McGuire (11)
Edward Feild CP Primary School, Kidlington

The Monster

What is it? It's heading for the fridge. It's getting closer, it's pulling something out of the fridge. It's beer, look, there's leftover cake on the table. He's heading to the Coke; he's turned around with his bald head. It's my dad, the beer monster.
'Go to bed Jasmin.'

Jasmin Sims (7)
Edward Feild CP Primary School, Kidlington

Tig Wars Episode 1, The Phantom Females

A short time ago on a playground far, far away, the lost war had begun. Females used their brutal nails to tear into our flesh. Fallen allies of mine had turned against me. The traitor rushed closer and hit me. I had lost.
'Tig!'
I was it, noo …

Tomos Hooper (11)
Edward Feild CP Primary School, Kidlington

Chemistry

I wonder if I would be good at chemistry. Let's have a go. I mix and combine two potions together but … uh-oh, take cover, she's going to blow! Then, I'm blasted up through the ceiling and later wake up in casualty! Maybe, I'll stick to physics, definitely physics.

Lucy Truman (10)
Edward Feild CP Primary School, Kidlington

Tears

Searing pain from my heart to the tip of my nail. It was dark. I didn't know what happened, maybe blood or maybe cracking bones. I knew it was like a sudden storm ripping out the life of a town but no, it was worse … I'd broken my nail!

Alison Brodie (11)
Edward Feild CP Primary School, Kidlington

Tiny Tales Southern Fiction

Pain

Snip, they came off seeming to pirouette onto the floor. I screamed, they were torturing me to the bone. Off fell some more. It felt like it was all going in slow motion. They passed me a mirror. I never knew beauty came with pain, I hate haircuts.

Julia Brain (11)
Edward Feild CP Primary School, Kidlington

Untitled

The door creaked open. Who was it? We were upstairs shaking in our beds. Peeking out of the door, a flicker of light flashed downstairs. Hearts pounding we carefully went step by step. As we reached the bottom it was quiet. *Bang!* The light turned on, Goldilocks was back!

Joe Howes (11)
Edward Feild CP Primary School, Kidlington

Forgotten

When Sam got home the doorbell rang. Who could that be? When he opened the door it was no human, it was an alien with a vampire shouting. 'Argh,' Sam screamed.
'Go careful!' the alien said as he took his mask off. 'Trick or treat?'

Jack Sims (10)
Edward Feild CP Primary School, Kidlington

The Monster

It was a dark stormy night and I was sitting in my living room. There was a knock at the door, a green spotty monster stood in the doorway.
'Argh,' I screamed. What was it?
'Happy Hallowe'en!' exclaimed the monster.

Bethany Hutson (11)
Edward Feild CP Primary School, Kidlington

Tiny Tales Southern Fiction

The True Story Of The Owl And The Pussycat

Went to sea in a pea-green boat. Wrong, a motorboat! Took some honey and plenty of money. It was a Happy Meal. And the pig? Nonsense! You don't get pigs with rings in their noses! It was a bull. Wasn't a banjo owl played? It was an electric guitar!

Geneviēve Tomes (9)
Edward Feild CP Primary School, Kidlington

The Crazy Witches

There were three new students in school that always messed about. They went to see the teacher and the witches had brought a ginger cat instead of a black cat. The witches tried a spell to change the cat black but instead it vanished and they were expelled!

Ellishia Chard (9)
Edward Feild CP Primary School, Kidlington

The Lion Or Is It?

I could hear it coming closer and closer, its paws scratching on the floor. I could hear its rough quiet growl as it walked on. But it will not find me. I am where no one can find me. Suddenly I hear silence, it has stopped.
'Abi, feed the cat!'

Abigail Teasdale (8)
Edward Feild CP Primary School, Kidlington

Lights Are Out

Dark, gloomy and deadly darkness. I was high up, I felt it. I had something in my hand; it was round with a screw on the end. I reached up to screw it in then suddenly the lights were on. I was the electrician changing the lightbulb.

Charlie Nutt (11)
Edward Feild CP Primary School, Kidlington

Tiny Tales Southern Fiction

The Monster Under My Bed

Boom! Bang! He's back again, the monster who crawls and dings. He is soft and black ready to attack. He is thirty-six and four. I know now, Max get out! You're only a cat from next door.

Connor Micallef (11)
Edward Feild CP Primary School, Kidlington

In Hiding

Running away. I think I've lost them. I'm visible in this bright beam. It's following me, marking me. I settle down hardly daring to breathe. Footsteps crunch around me ringing in my ears. They find me. 'Your turn to find us, our turn to hide!'

Zoe Hart (11)
Edward Feild CP Primary School, Kidlington

Untitled

Leaves surrounded me. I was alone. Some eyes appeared nearby. I trembled. Wind whirled in my ears. I was not alone. It then came, breathing warmly on my back, it yelled, 'I found you!' Ouch my ears hurt, someone save me from playing hide-and-seek.

Holly Lyford (11)
Edward Feild CP Primary School, Kidlington

Untitled

I walked upstairs, I heard a creaky sound coming from my room. I slowly opened the door. 'Finally, you're back,' croaked a voice. I turned the light on, a green-faced thing with cucumbers over its eyes, my heart thumping, it was my mum!

Maisie Siret (11)
Edward Feild CP Primary School, Kidlington

Alien

I'm falling into my bed a buzz, an alien is there. *Roar, gobble-gobble, zing*. He is purple. 'Help, help, help! I'm terrified.' He speaks English.
'I will eat chicken, sausages, pork.'
'Phew!' … 'You.'
'Harry I'm coming,' shouts Mum.
Ha, ha, ha, it's my big brother, oh no. *Gobble-gobble!*

Matthew Cunningham (8)
Edward Feild CP Primary School, Kidlington

What's That?

I took a step into the utility, I dare not turn around. There's a monster behind me! Panting and banging, getting louder and louder I began to cry, 'Argh! Help!' I turned around, not knowing I was even doing it and there it was … the dreaded washing machine!

Skye Turner (10)
Edward Feild CP Primary School, Kidlington

The Evil Thing

Ben was on the field playing. A light shone down onto the playground. A group of teachers came down to see what it was. There was a lamp post in the middle of the day? Suddenly a creature came and said funny words. 'Everybody get in a line.'

Kamran Afzal (10)
Edward Feild CP Primary School, Kidlington

Stanley The Stone Lion

Stanley was a stone statue. The children kept making a gigantic circle every time they went to the park. One day their circle made him come alive. He wasn't used to walking then suddenly he fell into the pond but we realised it was a suit made out of cloth.

Kieran Kilcoyne (8)
Edward Feild CP Primary School, Kidlington

The Evil Demon

In the room the noise was unbearable. They knew the demon was coming but when? Suddenly there was a footstep and lots more. They came closer then a sudden silence came. The demon came in and turned around. It was a teacher, 'Find your books,' said the teacher.

Toby Cole (9)
Edward Feild CP Primary School, Kidlington

When My Mum Went Camping

When my mum was younger she went camping with her parents and siblings. Apparently on the last day her and her siblings got up early, let their parents bed down when they were asleep. They giggled as they watched their mum and dad rolling off their airbed!

Natasha Owen (9)
Edward Feild CP Primary School, Kidlington

The Robber

Stacy sat silently on the sofa watching TV while someone was burgling her coins. She was still watching TV when suddenly she leapt up and started threatening him.
She realised that her horrible brother was just getting an apple from his packed lunch, 'Oh it's just you, Robert,' she said.

Chloe Pearce-Higgins (9)
Edward Feild CP Primary School, Kidlington

The Crazy Wizard

One day Firecrystal felt something on his back that sent shivers down his spine. He looked left and right but nobody was there! He touched a slimy thing crawling up, he stopped and there was a black and red centipede. Then he screamed, 'Argh!' and he was never seen again.

Georgia Allen (9)
Edward Feild CP Primary School, Kidlington

Loch Ness

Water bashed violently on the rusty boat. However water elsewhere was still as statues. Fiercely the boat shook, I was thrown like a dart sideways. Scottish, salty water in my mouth before I could yell for help. One small glimpse I saw, emerald monsters don't exist do they?

Alex Hedges (11)
Edward Feild CP Primary School, Kidlington

The Homework Chase

'Come here you, you didn't hand your homework in!' My evil teacher tripped and stumbled as she chased after me. She wore broken spectacles and had a potato-shaped nose. We were running down a long road.
'Argh!'
'Calm down honey, it was only a dream,' my mother said kindly.

Melissa Fry (9
Edward Feild CP Primary School, Kidlington

What Monster Am I Watching?

Something was moving, slowly, terribly slowly. Something was pedalling mildly, through murky slime. I watched breathless, ready to destroy. What could happen to me, any minute now? I was sat in the future Scotland experimenting the legend of some mystic creature. I was fearless but emotional, I'm a hero.

Scarlett Tomes (11)
Edward Feild CP Primary School, Kidlington

Zoo Animals Lost

Two girls went to the zoo and looked at the swans then at the penguins. The two girls went back to the car. They went home and they were back when they saw a monkey had escaped. The girls took it back to the zoo, the zookeeper said thank you.

Emma Gough (7)
Edward Feild CP Primary School, Kidlington

Sleeping

'Mummy, Mummy, the light went out, what has happened?'
'Sweetheart, it's OK, the lightbulb just went out.'
'OK.'
'Now go back to sleep.'
'OK … Mum, I can't get back to sleep.'
'I'll come up and read you a story.' I snuggled under the covers and fell fast asleep.

Katie Le Masurier (10)
First Tower School, St Helier

The Flood

I was deafened by a big *bang!* The road cracked and came up in an instant wave, the town was being flooded. I screamed, then the wave went down and I realised that it was my brother throwing stones at the rocks and the town was just my brilliant sandcastle.

Francesca Monticelli (10)
First Tower School, St Helier

Tiny Tales Southern Fiction

A Fright In The Night

'Mummy, Mummy.' I woke up with a fright. The lights were flickering. 'Where are you Mummy?'
'I'm in my room.'
'I can't see you Mummy.'
'I'm coming.'
'Mummy, I'm really scared.'
'OK, Mummy's coming.' The lights went on but all I could see was a black light. 'Mummy?'
'You're OK!'

Chloe Dashwood (10)
First Tower School, St Helier

Wake Up Call

It was Saturday morning. It was pitch-black. 'Argh!' I suddenly fell out of bed. I ran downstairs; Andy was stood on the table. All it was was a tiny spider. 'It's going to eat me the blinkin' thing!'

Nathan Samson (10)
First Tower School, St Helier

Tiny Tales Southern Fiction

Disappointment

Last Christmas I went to Madeira. I was so excited about Christmas Eve that I wrote Santa a letter. I asked him for roller skates but on Christmas Eve, no presents came from him. When I got home though there was my present from Santa, I was so relieved.

Isabella De Freitas (10)
First Tower School, St Helier

Jim Bob - My Dog

I was chased into the wood by a big monster; it's going to eat me. I was so scared! I hid in a tree. I closed my eyes then I heard a bang! I looked down, it was still there. Then I looked again, it was Jim Bob.

Jamie Hamilton (10)
First Tower School, St Helier

The Thing In My Bed

'Dad, there's something in my bed.' I was very scared, what could it be? A cockroach, it's ticklish. It might be a spider. My dad stormed in, he turned on the light but it was only a fly. My dad opened the window and the fly flew out.

Calum Fowler (10)
First Tower School, St Helier

The Caravan

The light went out, the caravan was in darkness but then a person walked towards me. It was a man I had never seen before. He took a tight grip of my hand and said, 'I am your father.' I was terrified.

Rosie Lee (10)
First Tower School, St Helier

Shields And Swords

I could feel the tension in the atmosphere. I was staring the enemy in the eye, he was staring back. Someone in my army shouted, 'Charge!' The war broke out.
I was about to swiftly cut the opposing leader when … 'Game over!' I had lost the bet, I played again.

Cole Courval (10)
First Tower School, St Helier

Spooky October

As I was heading to bed I heard a noise at the door then my son was shouting, 'Daddy, argh, aliens have invaded!'
I ran downstairs as fast as I could, I got my gun and as soon as I opened the door I heard, 'Trick or treat? Ha, ha!'

Jonathan Williams (10)
First Tower School, St Helier

Abracadabra

Abracadabra, my teeth were shaking, my hand went blue, all I could hear was whoo! I was going to disappear, the wand broke, I'm glad. My face just smiled, I got an evil look. My face went glum but I've still got that look.

Lucy Fraser (10)
First Tower School, St Helier

My Trip To School

I was walking alone for the first time. I tiptoed; I crept from tree to tree because I was so nervous. I was one road away from my school and I heard a rattle in the bush. I was freaked out! I turned around and it was … a ginger cat!

Gaganpreet Bangar (9)
Hambrough Primary School, Southall

Catopia's Angels VS Dogmastic Fairydog Mother

There was a world with three suns, different sizes where the sky is pink clouds and stars. Catangels rule the place. Georgina the catangel went for a little fly in the sky. The fairydog mother went to Catopia for a little visit and wrecked Catopia and the solar system.

Safiya Ali (10)
Hambrough Primary School, Southall

Dolls

I heard a creak and little footsteps; I had to open my eyes. I couldn't believe it, my dolls were moving! I had to call my elder sister, they were marching and they were coming towards me. Then I heard my mum, I woke up, I was dreaming!

Divya Thankaraj (10)
Hambrough Primary School, Southall

The Lost Princess

They found her huddled up by a tree with a crown. The police had to investigate as the crown looked real. The king was asked if he recognised the crown. Surprisingly he did. He was presented to her, he was the dad of the girl. They lived happily ever after.

Alisha Janjua (10)
Hambrough Primary School, Southall

Spookness - Approach

An old house which had a skeleton was guarded by ghosts and souls. But Jack wasn't scared, but one day he saw that house and went in but didn't see anything. He went inside a room and saw a box open in which he saw a bone, Jack ran away.

Zionita Rathod (10)
Hambrough Primary School, Southall

Tiny Tales Southern Fiction

The Mean Aliens

Once there was a robber who went into a spaceship. He wanted to do whatever he wanted. He got caught by a bunch of aliens. They swapped his brain with an alien's brain. When he got back on Earth, people thought he was very, very weird.

Shivani Ohari (9)
Hambrough Primary School, Southall

Jessica's Broken Leg

Jessica was riding her bike. She fell off it and broke her leg. She arrived at the hospital. When it was better people came from fabulous houses and gave her presents. Her mum put them somewhere safe and no one could have them to keep. Jessica enjoyed playing with them.

Naurane Asif (8)
Hambrough Primary School, Southall

Tiny Tales Southern Fiction

The World's Best Birthday Party

When I returned from school my house looked haunted. It was like a vampire lived there. I tip-toped inside, it was darker than outdoors. As I opened my bedroom door …
'Surprise!'
It was my birthday and my present was a unicorn.
'Thanks everyone and what a fabulous birthday present.'

Hamza Butt (8)
Hambrough Primary School, Southall

The Birthday Surprise

When I came home Dad and Mum said they'd be home for my birthday. I am sure they must be here. Then, I heard a noise. I didn't know where it came from.
'Surprise!' gasped Mum.
'Happy birthday,' said Dad, 'let's cut the cake. Come on, let's go Lizzie.'
'OK.'

Shabana Mussa (7)
Hambrough Primary School, Southall

Magical Island

On an island lived fairies with magic. One was named Ruby. She was very sweet. In the morning evil goblins arrived with guns. Every fairy woke up with a shock. They used their magic to defeat them, unfortunately they didn't succeed, no one went to the island ever again.

Fatima Ali (8)
Hambrough Primary School, Southall

The Lost Gem

One night there was a wizard walking through an alley. Suddenly the wizard slipped in a puddle and a gem dropped out his pocket. He tried using his magic but he could only use it in daytime. He waited till morning, chanted the magic words and found his gem.

Jigar Santilal
Hambrough Primary School, Southall

The Lost Pearl

One ordinary, frightening day a wizard from the planet Peru appeared from a magical dustbin. Suddenly he was shocked at something so bright as the twinkling stars. He was angry at its presence because he was afraid of darkness. His sword wasn't shining so the wizard put the pearl in.

Ramanjit Marway (9)
Hambrough Primary School, Southall

The Wizard's Lost Gem

One dark night when the moon was shining on a snowy cliff top, a wizard was born. He trained and trained until he was prepared to fight. Unfortunately one day the wizard lost his gem, so he bolted into the black hole and found his precious glowing gem of life.

Rajan Mann (9)
Hambrough Primary School, Southall

Deserted House

There was a teenage rebel boy who was eager to enter a deserted house. Then stumbling he dropped into a trap. Dracula captured him! The boy was extremely terrified that he shouted, 'I'm terrified, okay!' Then the boy wished to leave and it happened. The boy left unhurt.

Preetam Virdee (9)
Hambrough Primary School, Southall

One Cuddly Toy

One day a princess called Rhianna was walking down the street with Vicky. They went inside the gateway, Vicky had a cuddly toy. Suddenly they froze and the toy was much bigger, they unfroze, they were running and running, the toy caught them and hugged them.

Sarika Chauhan (9)
Hambrough Primary School, Southall

The Deadly Potion

In the market place of Scarbot lived a father. He was an inventor and was very good at making potions. One day he decided to make a deadly potion. He wanted to test the potion so he tried it out on his daughter. Unfortunately when she tried it she died!

Ruth Ladani (8)
Hambrough Primary School, Southall

The Evil Toy

'Mum, I want a toy,' cried Rajandeep.
'Sure,' said Rajandeep's mum. They walked outside and attempted to find a shop. They couldn't find a shop but then they found a toy in the water and took it.
When Rajandeep was done playing, the toy came alive and killed them!

Rajinder Chana (8)
Hambrough Primary School, Southall

Tiny Tales Southern Fiction

The King

'I've really had enough,' said the king. 'I am going to get my clothes, run away to a secret tower and never come out.'
Years later his brother, who was in the forest, came to the tower. He went inside and found the king!

Marya Razzaq (9)
Hambrough Primary School, Southall

Untitled

'I crept towards a cave lurking inside this huge forest. Trees towered above the dark opening in the rock. I stepped inside. The walls encrusted with bone. I could taste the revolting smell. My heart drummed. The gold was in there somewhere but I never found it!' laughed Dad.

Sam Robins (10)
Kintbury St Mary's CE Primary School, Kintbury

One Day

One day I went to the park with my friends. I spotted a letter with my name on. I looked around no one was there. In a sudden flash I saw a ghost. I ran, it followed. It called my name over and over. I ran away.

Julia Thorp (10)
Kintbury St Mary's CE Primary School, Kintbury

Monster In The Cave

I'm going to slay what they call 'the cave monster'! On my way there I met a man who gave me a small matchbox. When I got there the monster emerged and knocked me to the ground. I lit a match and threw it. Then the cave burnt down.

Toby Chandler (10)
Kintbury St Mary's CE Primary School, Kintbury

The Parcel

I was at the park and I saw a parcel. It had my grandma's handwriting on it. She died a year ago. I opened it. Inside was a lucky charm. What shall I do with it? She died a year ago. She must be a ghost. Maybe she was scared.

Louise Fell (10)
Kintbury St Mary's CE Primary School, Kintbury

The Weird And Peculiar

Fineon, Fred and Yuna traveled from Fynn to Cornelia. On the way we had a boss called the Oneymite. We beat it with six level seven magic blizzards. Then I set off to Cornelia when fifty goblins stole the diamonds that had our magic in it. Then *whoosh!* They vanished.

Jack Moore (10)
Kintbury St Mary's CE Primary School, Kintbury

The Wonder River

A very spoilt boy wandered up a path which went up a hill. He went to get a drink from a stream and drank it. Suddenly he slipped and fell.
'You are in the Wander River,' a voice called. He saw his past life then awoke as a polite boy.

Benjamin Grey (10)
Kintbury St Mary's CE Primary School, Kintbury

Learning Lines

I take a big breath and start. 'Wind whistles through the gaps in the window. Cold air blows out candles in a puff, and door joints creak. I wrap my arms around me. As I sit down, my legs shake together … ummm.'
'Cut,' said the director. 'Learn your lines tonight.'

Saskia Marshall (10)
Kintbury St Mary's CE Primary School, Kintbury

Tiny Tales Southern Fiction

My Nan's Bulldog

I was about to open the door to the cupboard when I heard a strange growling noise. 'Grrrr!' it said.
'Arrrgh!' I screamed. I was afraid to open it after what I'd just heard but I did. The noise was only my nan's dog. I wish I wasn't so afraid of bulldogs.

Sinead Graham (10)
Kintbury St Mary's CE Primary School, Kintbury

The Football Match

Jimmy stood there freezing. Suddenly the ball came towards him. He kicked it away randomly. 'Jimmy,' shouted Tim. Jimmy felt awful. Anyway it was the second half now. He ran towards the other players, tackled them and shot. He had scored the winning goal. Tim told Jimmy he's great!

Amy Sidhu (10)
Kintbury St Mary's CE Primary School, Kintbury

Tiny Tales Southern Fiction

The Big Accident

One day in 2000, on Friday in a bank a woman called Tanya was going down an escalator which was jam-packed. A man was so desperate to get down, he pushed her and she caught her hand in the side of it. Ever since she hates going down escalators.

Kieren Phipps (11)
Kintbury St Mary's CE Primary School, Kintbury

Alone

The floorboards creaked and Jackie's heart thumped. She crept along the hallway to the phone and dialed her mum. No answer. She cried. Then the door burst open. In came her mum.
'Where were you? I told you to meet at Sally's,' her mum told her.

Chloe Boulter (11)
Kintbury St Mary's CE Primary School, Kintbury

Tiny Tales Southern Fiction

Scarlet's Secret - Almost Discovered

Scarlet overslept working late - 9.30. She arrived at school, opened her desk, her diary was open! Someone must know her secret - understanding animals. Melissa confronted her. She'd read it and now threatened to tell everyone unless Scarlet taught Melissa her skill. Together Scarlet and the animals trapped Melissa - forever.

Sky Caves (9)
Kintbury St Mary's CE Primary School, Kintbury

Shadow Walker

Silence. Not a movement in the garden … Then something stirred amongst the bushes and a lean figure crept past the overgrown trees; a silhouette in the moonlight. He seemed to be heading towards the palace. Suddenly, a moonbeam glinted through the dark trees, revealing a silver knife in his hand.

Gee-Heon Kim (11)
Lady Eleanor Holles Junior School, Hampton Hill

Mum's Sidekick Is A Sprout

I'd bitten off more than I could chew. The situation grew desperate as my jaw started to ache. With all my might I forced it down to the place where it should never belong. The stench overtook me as I stared my tormentor in the eyes.
I low I hate sprouts!

Emily Smith (10)
Lady Eleanor Holles Junior School, Hampton Hill

Anticipation

Opening the creaky door there were spiderwebs everywhere, I had never been in the dilapidated house before. I was sure I had seen him creeping around inside. I heard a creak. Nervously, I turned around. There he was, sitting there. It was him. I had found Chester my adventurous cat.

Lucinda Smith (11)
Lady Eleanor Holles Junior School, Hampton Hill

Swallowed Deep

I felt my feet being swallowed by the damp slippery sand. My hands trickled against the crystal waters of the tropical island. I sank … slowly … steadily until I couldn't breathe. It was only then I realised that I was the one who was supposed to die. They had succeeded … No!

Maria Griston (11)
Lady Eleanor Holles Junior School, Hampton Hill

The Calm Before The Storm

Everyone was dressed in black. The vicar's voice was drowned out by the rain. I wasn't listening anyway.
I could hear a rumbling sound. Suddenly, a flash of lightning vividly illuminated a shadow. I had never seen it before. Then it vanished, leaving me, only the rain blurring my vision.

Nicole Quah (11)
Lady Eleanor Holles Junior School, Hampton Hill

The Nightingale

In the dead of night, Kate crept through the undergrowth. She was listening for a nightingale's song. Suddenly, she heard a sound that made her return to the house and jump into bed.
Kate realised the sound had been that of the nightingale's call that she had been searching for.

Rosamund Downer (10)
Lady Eleanor Holles Junior School, Hampton Hill

Gladiator

The sickening noise from the bloodthirsty crowd was deafening. An anxious prisoner paced his cage, waiting for the moment. The bars slid back and the prisoner leapt into the blazing sun. Too late. A gladiator's spear caught him in the chest. The majestic lion fell to the ground, dead.

Imogen Thwaites (11)
Lady Eleanor Holles Junior School, Hampton Hill

Mini Saga

I stared at the letter. A torrent of despair engulfed my body as my eyelids clamped together. It wasn't a dream. My heart pounded desperately whilst a shiver violently flew down my spine. Sweat cascaded down as a single tear trickled down my face. I couldn't believe it. Suicide?

Monica Gupta (11)
Lady Eleanor Holles Junior School, Hampton Hill

Phobias!

I've never been so terrified in my life. As I glanced downwards, I saw clusters of ant-sized people. I recognised a swarm to be my mates who were all encouragingly shouting, 'Jump!' Slowly, I clamped my eyes shut, took a deep breath and leapt onto the zip wire. Success!

Kirsten Chaplin (11)
Lady Eleanor Holles Junior School, Hampton Hill

Tiny Tales Southern Fiction

Freeze

I was walking the same usual boring way home, but something didn't seem quite right. Everyone seemed to be avoiding me. It was getting dark. I swung my shoulder bag round to get my keys. I felt cold icy air on my neck. The hook-handed man was waiting. Waiting …

Ellie Roberts (11)
Lady Eleanor Holles Junior School, Hampton Hill

Mini Saga

I started to climb the dark Victorian staircase, stairs creaking with every tread. Darkness overwhelmed me. Sensing a presence on the stairs, my heart started to pound. My palms started sweating as I crept up the remaining stairs. Suddenly, Dad shouted, 'Just changing the light bulb on the landing!'
Dad!

Anna Stuart (11)
Lady Eleanor Holles Junior School, Hampton Hill

The Lion Man

Once there was a man and he had a lion park. He had over 40 Siberian tigers and 6 rare white lions. He lived in New Zealand and had a very close relationship with them. He had the chance of a lifetime to get so close to them.

Joshua Daulton (11)
Littledown School, Slough

Vampires

The two blood-covered vampires moved to their next target. Inside, an old lady sat knitting away. The doorbell rang. The vampires got ready to sink their teeth into their next victim. They were ready. The old lady opened the door.
'Trick or treat?' Anne and Ryan shouted together.

Pratham Mishra (9)
Loddon Primary School, Earley

Tiny Tales Southern Fiction

The Ghost Train

It was a gloomy, foggy day. Jade was on the ghost train. The train was going on forever. She heard squeaks then screams and suddenly, she saw bats in the distance. 'Argh!' she screamed. There was no one else on the train except for her. She looked around in fright …

Urvi Bihani (9)
Loddon Primary School, Earley

Untitled

When Sam got there his dreams drowned because it was better than going swimming or anything you could think of. It's cool, fun, scary, robotic trampolining, trampolining with all your friends is a dream come true, also when you jump on the trampoline you get transported to your best dream!

Mouadjul Miah (8)
Loddon Primary School, Earley

Anticipation

Opening the creaky door there were spiderwebs everywhere, I had never been in the dilapidated house before. I was sure I had seen him creeping around inside. I heard a creak. Nervously, I turned around. There he was, sitting there. It was him. I had found Chester my adventurous cat.

Lucinda Smith (11)
Lady Eleanor Holles Junior School, Hampton Hill

Swallowed Deep

I felt my feet being swallowed by the damp slippery sand. My hands trickled against the crystal waters of the tropical island. I sank … slowly … steadily until I couldn't breathe. It was only then I realised that I was the one who was supposed to die. They had succeeded … No!

Maria Griston (11)
Lady Eleanor Holles Junior School, Hampton Hill

Tiny Tales Southern Fiction

The Calm Before The Storm

Everyone was dressed in black. The vicar's voice was drowned out by the rain. I wasn't listening anyway.
I could hear a rumbling sound. Suddenly, a flash of lightning vividly illuminated a shadow. I had never seen it before. Then it vanished, leaving me, only the rain blurring my vision.

Nicole Quah (11)
Lady Eleanor Holles Junior School, Hampton Hill

Mum's Sidekick Is A Sprout

I'd bitten off more than I could chew. The situation grew desperate as my jaw started to ache. With all my might I forced it down to the place where it should never belong. The stench overtook me as I stared my tormentor in the eyes.
How I hate sprouts!

Emily Smith (10)
Lady Eleanor Holles Junior School, Hampton Hill

Untitled

When Sam got there his dreams drowned because it was better than going swimming or anything you could think of. It's cool, fun, scary, robotic trampolining, trampolining with all your friends is a dream come true, also when you jump on the trampoline you get transported to your best dream!

Mouadjul Miah (8)
Loddon Primary School, Earley

The Ghost Train

It was a gloomy, foggy day. Jade was on the ghost train. The train was going on forever. She heard squeaks then screams and suddenly, she saw bats in the distance. 'Argh!' she screamed. There was no one else on the train except for her. She looked around in fright …

Urvi Bihani (9)
Loddon Primary School, Earley

Vampires

The two blood-covered vampires moved to their next target. Inside, an old lady sat knitting away. The doorbell rang. The vampires got ready to sink their teeth into their next victim. They were ready. The old lady opened the door.
'Trick or treat?' Anne and Ryan shouted together.

Pratham Mishra (9)
Loddon Primary School, Earley

The Lion Man

Once there was a man and he had a lion park. He had over 40 Siberian tigers and 6 rare white lions. He lived in New Zealand and had a very close relationship with them. He had the chance of a lifetime to get so close to them.

Joshua Daulton (11)
Littledown School, Slough

Mini Saga

I started to climb the dark Victorian staircase, stairs creaking with every tread. Darkness overwhelmed me. Sensing a presence on the stairs, my heart started to pound. My palms started sweating as I crept up the remaining stairs. Suddenly, Dad shouted, 'Just changing the light bulb on the landing!'
Dad!

Anna Stuart (11)
Lady Eleanor Holles Junior School, Hampton Hill

Freeze

I was walking the same usual boring way home, but something didn't seem quite right. Everyone seemed to be avoiding me. It was getting dark. I swung my shoulder bag round to get my keys. I felt cold icy air on my neck. The hook-handed man was waiting. Waiting …

Ellie Roberts (11)
Lady Eleanor Holles Junior School, Hampton Hill

Phobias!

I've never been so terrified in my life. As I glanced downwards, I saw clusters of ant-sized people. I recognised a swarm to be my mates who were all encouragingly shouting, 'Jump!' Slowly, I clamped my eyes shut, took a deep breath and leapt onto the zip wire. Success!

Kirsten Chaplin (11)
Lady Eleanor Holles Junior School, Hampton Hill

Mini Saga

I stared at the letter. A torrent of despair engulfed my body as my eyelids clamped together. It wasn't a dream. My heart pounded desperately whilst a shiver violently flew down my spine. Sweat cascaded down as a single tear trickled down my face. I couldn't believe it. Suicide?

Monica Gupta (11)
Lady Eleanor Holles Junior School, Hampton Hill

Gladiator

The sickening noise from the bloodthirsty crowd was deafening. An anxious prisoner paced his cage, waiting for the moment. The bars slid back and the prisoner leapt into the blazing sun. Too late. A gladiator's spear caught him in the chest. The majestic lion fell to the ground, dead.

Imogen Thwaites (11)
Lady Eleanor Holles Junior School, Hampton Hill

Tiny Tales Southern Fiction

The Nightingale

In the dead of night, Kate crept through the undergrowth. She was listening for a nightingale's song. Suddenly, she heard a sound that made her return to the house and jump into bed.
Kate realised the sound had been that of the nightingale's call that she had been searching for.

Rosamund Downer (10)
Lady Eleanor Holles Junior School, Hampton Hill

The Bad News

The house was dark. A little too dark. Georgia opened the door but then she heard voices crying, crying in the living room. She ran out the door crying. She stared through the window, she wasn't too happy. She saw Mum glaring at her in a sad way. She knew!

Sophie Busby (9)
Loddon Primary School, Earley

The Bull And Horse

The wind was up. I was cold. The rider on the horse was wearing red. Smoke came out of the bull's nostrils as the horse kicked the sand. Suddenly the bull charged at the horse. The horse dodged out the way. It was amazing the moment it happened.

Hannah Pollard (9)
Loddon Primary School, Earley

Untitled

Crawling through the slimy sewers, heart racing, I was nearly there in the open, but the monster rapidly gained on me. I fumbled and tripped reaching out still grasping the jewel. I lunged for the entrance. I was there but Monster Mum had got me.
'Game over, bathtime!' chuckled Mum.

Esther Bilton (10)
Loddon Primary School, Earley

Lost

She shivered, as Katie opened her deep blue eyes to a gloomy-looking room. She stared at the window not knowing what to think. Suddenly she saw the black door open, leading her way into the next room. There she was, her mother, saying it was all a dream.

Ishwari Sharma (10)
Loddon Primary School, Earley

Sneaky Burglar

I got home quickly and Sarah my sister was there waiting on the doorstep shivering with fright. I called to her. 'Lost your key?'
She said she left it under the doormat but it wasn't there!
We got in and looked in the bedroom, a burglar stared at us!

Megan Cadman (10)
Loddon Primary School, Earley

A Bad Dream

Suddenly the door slammed closed. I was trapped in an old creepy castle. I tried to open the door, it was stuck. It felt like a wizard had cast a spell on me so I couldn't move. The next day was perfectly normal. Was it a dream?

Emma Billington (10)
Loddon Primary School, Earley

The Dummy

Bobby, a two-year-old toddler, that had just learnt to walk and talk, wanted a new dummy. So he waddled to his dad and screamed, 'Dummy, dummy, me want dummy!' His dad looked at him joyfully. 'Here,' chirped his dad, giving it to him. 'Ahh, old dummy!' Bobby groaned.

Leah Martins (10)
Loddon Primary School, Earley

Scared!

Once a girl called Lily lived in a town called Scaryville where there was a house that no one dared to enter. So Lily decided to go in. The house had been left. There were cobwebs everywhere, then she heard a terrifying noise so she ran home scared!

Chloe Beckett (10)
Loddon Primary School, Earley

The Man In The Passageway

6192: A man discovered a passageway. In the passageway were dead trees and dead people. Something rumbled in the bush. It was a walking skeleton. More and more came. He was scared. The wall came crushing in. A woman looked down from the ceiling. She lowered a rope. He climbed.

Benjamin Mitchelmore (8)
St John's RC Primary School, Banbury

Pre-Historic Adventure

One day at school I discovered a secret passage to another dimension: Prehistoric Sweety Island. Everything chocolate! Wow! Even the volcanic lava was chocolate! I had an awesome time. Suddenly a T-rex bashed through all the chocolate trees. I was terrified but the T-rex had past. I was safe.

Joe Mates (7)
St John's RC Primary School, Banbury

Untitled

It was a snowy day and Hayley was sitting inside feeling very bored so she went outside to play in the snow. Hayley hated the snow. The snow suddenly melted away and Hayley lay down to sunbathe. It was the best day of Hayley's life! And it stayed that way.

Eleanor Claridge (8)
St John's RC Primary School, Banbury

Untitled

On the thirtieth of June 2002 a worker went into a castle to take pictures for the newspaper. Then one of the guards took him away into cells. He stayed there for the rest of his life until the Queen set him free. Then he had a big party.

Matthew Cummings-Coules (8)
St John's RC Primary School, Banbury

Scary Hallway

I walked down the hallway, looking in every direction. 'Zap, you're dead, you can't kill me.' Then I felt an ice-cold shiver run down my spine. It jumped out at me and hit me. Everything went black and two words appeared, they said *game over.*

Tom Mulcahy (10)
St Mary's Catholic Primary School, Maidenhead

The Terror Swing

It was horrible, swinging me from back to front, launching me into the cold winter air. Shoving me forward and backwards like a rocking horse going mad. Then I realised it was just my fear of swings. I wish I could overcome my fear of swings, oh I wish.

Zack Minter (10)
St Mary's Catholic Primary School, Maidenhead

Tiny Tales Southern Fiction

The Adventure

This was the moment, the moment I have been waiting for, the most thrilling adventure in history. Just a few more steps, two more steps, one more step.
At last I was there at the petrol station! My Mars ice cream awaits me!

Victoria Paul (11)
St Mary's Catholic Primary School, Maidenhead

Trapped

I looked left, then right. Up, then down. I was trapped.
'There is no escape,' a rasping voice whispered softly.
I thought *run, run now. You can do it.* But I was paralysed. Then a gnarled hand reached out from behind. sweat glistened on my brow.
'You're it!' sang Amy.

Jack Cooper (11)
St Mary's Catholic Primary School, Maidenhead

The Angry Beast

The beast was coming slowly through the front door. Then silent footsteps on the ground to the first step. Up the steps it came, angrily but silently walking through the upstairs hallway. Then I heard it opening the door to my room. 'Go to bed Elisa, now!' Mum shouted angrily.

Elisa Di-Rosa (11)
St Mary's Catholic Primary School, Maidenhead

Cindebella

Cindebella was walking her usual walk when she heard a funny swishing noise. She started panting faster and faster. Then she took a deep breath and ran for her life. Suddenly she stopped and looked over her shoulder and all that was there was her sweet little cat prince.

Shannon Jarnak (11)
St Mary's Catholic Primary School, Maidenhead

Tiny Tales Southern Fiction

Under Attack

Cold metal bullets are being violently hurled at me, and they're tearing away at my arm, leg and knee.
But do not worry my friend, for these bullets shall cause no pain for they're only tiny harmless drops of wet horrible rain.

Oscar Rutishauser-Mills (11)
St Mary's Catholic Primary School, Maidenhead

Untitled

I stepped in, wiping cobwebs from my face. My legs shivered, my head banged, I heard a creak. I turned around and saw a black figure in the distance. Suddenly I fell with a thump, knocking my head. I then wished I had never been so adventurous.

Bryony Mulholland (11)
St Mary's Catholic Primary School, Maidenhead

Untitled

'Can I buy it? It's so sweet.'
'Okay then,' Mum sighed.
Finally I had a fluffy white bunny. I ran with it to my room. It had tiny ears. It started staring at me! I stroked it. It bit me! Suddenly its head turned blood-red. It wasn't a bunny …

Luis Homer (11)
St Mary's Catholic Primary School, Maidenhead

War

Tim clawed his way through the sand. *Bang!* Bullets sailed everywhere. Screams could be heard. *Boom!* A bomb exploded. A voice rang out, 'Run for it!'

Tim dashed towards the ship. He scrambled inside as the ship departed. He'd made it. He would see his family again. He was safe.

Ryan Manuel (11)
St Mary's Catholic Primary School, Maidenhead

I Was There

I was there in the corner of my room shivering. I could see the bright glow of the thing from under the door, the monster had eight tentacles that wrapped around the door, it broke. The eight-legged glowing creature was there standing ready to attack.
'It's dinner time hee!'

Max Barnes (11)
St Mary's Catholic Primary School, Maidenhead

Lost And Found

My hamster, I didn't think he would be alive, not now, not after days without any food or water. Going upstairs I saw something scurry quickly across the landing. I saw him scratching at the woodwork and chased him back into his cage. *Phew,* I hope that never happens again.

Isabelle Smith (11)
St Mary's Catholic Primary School, Maidenhead

Tiny Tales Southern Fiction

The Marbles Under The Bed

The eyes look at me, as I move closer. Its sinister eyes look like a bat in a cave. I wish I wasn't so scared of the marbles under the bed.

Megan McCaffrey (11)
St Mary's Catholic Primary School, Maidenhead

The Stormy Climb

The storm was approaching, the rain was pounding me hard on the head. The teachers and pupils were doing all they could to get me to safety. The branch was strong but it wasn't strong enough. I was sure I was going to fall in the next minute or so.

Israr Akhtar (11)
St Mary's Catholic Primary School, Maidenhead

The Not So Evil Monster

The creaking noise was getting closer and closer. Suddenly, my bedroom door flew open and a huge, hairy monster jumped on me. As I turned my bedside light on, hoping it would scare the horrible monster, I realised the beast was Rufus my dog, licking my face madly.

Katie Greet (11)
St Mary's Catholic Primary School, Maidenhead

The Mysterious Wardrobe

Dreadful screams were coming from the black, dark wardrobe. My face turned white from fright. Was that an alien? It talked in an extremely strange way. The extraordinary language was very familiar. I listened carefully … then I remembered the high-pitched voice, 'Help! Mom, Mat trapped me in his wardrobe!'

Mateusz Wzietal (11)
St Mary's Catholic Primary School, Maidenhead

Untitled

It was the middle of the night. Sarah heard a creaking sound coming from downstairs. She thought it was a burglar so she crept downstairs. Then she turned the light on and screamed *argh* … but then she realised it was only her dad getting a drink of water.

Isabella Williams (11)
St Mary's Catholic Primary School, Maidenhead

Good Morning

'Come on!' bellowed a huge voice. Charlie sweated, his eyes started to water. He knew that what he was about to do was potentially hazardous. He opened one eye and squinted. All he could see was an eternal darkness. Suddenly a short blinding light was upon him. 'Rise and shine!'

Callum Edwards (11)
St Mary's Catholic Primary School, Maidenhead

The Terrier

It was running around like a terrier. It crashed to the ground and smashed a glass vase. It came up to me and breathed heavily on my neck. It sensed fear. Suddenly it pounced on me. 'Can we go to the sweet shop please?' screamed my little brother.

James Herron (10)
St Mary's Catholic Primary School, Maidenhead

The Beast

The door downstairs swung open and slammed shut with such force the house seemed to shake. The whole world's nightmares had come true. The terrible creature was here. The beast had entered its lair. A blood-curdling thing happened to me, my brother had come home from summer camp.

Robert Nash (11)
St Mary's Catholic Primary School, Maidenhead

Boo!

I looked everywhere I could have looked, upstairs and downstairs but I still couldn't find what I was looking for. Then, I went into my room. The lights were off, I heard something move.
Click, the lights went on.
'Boo!' something said.
It was my annoying little brother James.

Juno Tejeda (11)
St Mary's Catholic Primary School, Maidenhead

The Mouse House

Well this is the story about four mice, a mother, a father and two children. They are called Jane and Jack and they all lived in a house together. Jane was going to her friend's house. Jack was upset because he was not going. He had to do boring homework.

Kayleigh Ramsay (9)
Stoke Row CE Primary School, Henley-on-Thames

Drowning

I slipped. The water came over my chin, my nose, my eyes … I slipped lower and it covered my head.
Mustn't breathe the water in, I thought.
My lungs burned.
It grew dark. I had to breathe … Just then Mum lifted me out.
'Bathtime's over,' she said.

Mary Lobo (8)
Stoke Row CE Primary School, Henley-on-Thames

Volcano Struggle

Nick struggled up the hot volcano. He sighed with relief, the emerald was there! It was the emerald of immortality. He heard a faint tap. He turned. Saw nothing. Then, out of the volcanic mist, a hand reached out to the unwary Nick. Whose hand is it?

Kieran Tang (11)
The Batt CE School, Witney

The Poor Dog

One sunny day there was a little dog with no tail. He was a lonely dog. No one liked him. Everyone thought they were better than him. But he became the nicest dog ever. He was a fire dog. He saved people. All his friends said sorry to him.

Kirby Henderson-Sowerby (11)
The Batt CE School, Witney

Take That

I fell asleep. Suddenly some giant flowers appeared. They made me work as a slave for three years! They all chanted work until I got my grips together, found some flower food and sprayed it over them! I found my way back home nice and safely using a magic portal!

Connie Manning (11)
The Batt CE School, Witney

Tiny Tales Southern Fiction

What Is It?

What is it, I don't know, strolling along? Is it … a … monkey swinging from tree to tree from China? Is it a … buzz buzz bee taking nectar for tea? Yes or no! No! it's a … yummy, scrummy, tasty, satisfactory sausage with a cap, some gloves too … for my tummy!

Charlotte Roberts (11)
The Batt CE School, Witney

The Battle

Once, a long time ago there was a big battle between two men. Each man had an army of about fifty and one day they had a fierce battle. Eventually one of the men ran away from the battle and the other man was left there laughing.

Christopher Macdonald (10)
The Batt CE School, Witney

Tiny Tales Southern Fiction

The Killer Jellybean

One day, Danny Wellgood went down to the sweet shop to get Maltesers when out of nowhere the jellybean ghost appeared. The next day Danny was in a hole. He had choked on a jellybean.

Ash Myall (10)
The Batt CE School, Witney

A Life Change

A race. A crash. Calvin's life raced before his eyes as he walked down a tunnel. The light at the end was sooo tempting. He walked through. He was falling. Suddenly everything went black. It was then Calvin realised the difference between life and death.

Joslyn Beadle (10)
The Batt CE School, Witney

The Haunted House

One day a man went into a haunted house. When he got there he heard a high-pitched scream.
Then he walked a bit further, something grabbed him! He was getting strangled! He was dying! He turned around. It was a ghost! He saw one glimpse, then died.

Taylor Lee (10)
The Batt CE School, Witney

Crystal Clear

Thousands of years ago a magic crystal lay beneath the snow. A penguin dug it up. The crystal was so cold that it shattered into pieces. From that day forward the penguins searched for the pieces to the legendary clear magic crystal!

Bethany Knight (10)
The Batt CE School, Witney

The Bloodthirsty Event

One day a teenager went swimming in the blue open sea. All of a sudden something was coming closer and closer until a gush of blood came running across the beach. She was never seen again.

Lydia Locke (10)
The Batt CE School, Witney

The Pirate Who Met A Shark (Sharky)

There once was a pirate that sailed the seas in a one man boat with cannons. He met a shark. 'He's going to eat me!' shouted the pirate. Sharky leapt out of the water. Pirate ducked and Sharky felled the mast.

Edward Longden (10)
The Batt CE School, Witney

Magical Shell

There was a girl called Tilly and she is very pretty and nice. Tilly and her mum and dad went to the beach with Tilly's uncle. Suddenly, Tilly went for a walk to collect some shells. She found a colourful shell. Tilly kept it and she felt very protected.

Ysabela Torres (10)
The Batt CE School, Witney

Tragically

I knew this would end in tragedy. It was the week before Christmas. I was in Iceland on holiday going up a ski lift. It was a painful ride but we got to the top. My skis were on and I took off, but did I know they had snapped?

William Keating (10)
The Batt CE School, Witney

Tiny Tales Southern Fiction

The Best Game Of Golf Ever

This was my first ever game of golf. I put my ball on the blue tee. I swung back and hit the ball. My ball landed in the rough on a treasure map. When I found the spot I discovered a box of jewels and gold.

Harry Hamblin (9)
The Batt CE School, Witney

The Surprise

Sophie heard a noise. She thought it was a scary beast so she went downstairs and she found out it was her dog chewing on some roast beef. So Sophie went back to bed and rested her sweet head.

Michael Phelps (10)
The Batt CE School, Witney

The Graveyard

In shadows dark and gravestones old a skeleton wakes, glistening white sits up, an aged mouth smiles a sickly smile. Now he steps up, moves closer. A cold air drawing breath, a slimy ancient hand stretched out ready to grab your throat …

Carenza Glithero (10)
The Batt CE School, Witney

The Haunted House

As we crept along the floorboards we heard a kitchen cupboard open. 'Who is that?' I whispered as our big brother Dylan ushered us up the stairs. But then I heard an 'Argh'. Amy turned to see Dylan being dragged helplessly across the hall towards the kitchen to die!

Georgina Holliday (10)
The Batt CE School, Witney

Tiny Tales Southern Fiction

The Creature

It was there, it was asleep but it was still scary. Sarah crept towards it making sure she wasn't going to wake it up. Then it moved. Sarah stopped. She looked to see if it moved again but it didn't.
Suddenly, 'Sarah get out of bed now!' shouted her mum.

Lucy Nobes (10)
The Batt CE School, Witney

The Great Fire

There was a great fire. It burned down the whole city. The fire brigade was called. They saved the city. There was a movie star who died in the fire. Her career was taken over by a man named Joe.

Rosie Meredith (10)
The Batt CE School, Witney

Tiny Tales Southern Fiction

The Bed Monster

'Boo!' said the monster.
'Who are you?' asked the boy.
'I am the bed monster and I make children have nightmares and bad dreams.'
'But that's not very nice,' returned the boy.
'Well, it wasn't very nice of you to break your bed on my head!'
'Goodbye,' said the boy.

Fraser Stokes (10)
The Batt CE School, Witney

A Strange Adventure

The space rocket landed on the moon. Everyone piled out, they stared at the stars. Suddenly aliens jumped out in red, yellow and green. A speck of skin showed, then they realised that it was a surprise space party.

Holly Warne (10)
The Batt CE School, Witney

Tiny Tales Southern Fiction

Alien Attack

The alien spaceship landed. Bob saw it and reached for the gun. He got it and aimed it at the reactor. Bob shot once at it and missed. He shot it again and *boom.* He had saved the world.

Marcus Camm (10)
The Batt CE School, Witney

The Ssss Noise

I heard a *ssss* noise. I went upstairs two by two. Creak went the floorboards. I walked into my mum's room and the noise got louder and it was my mum putting on body spray.

Jessica Berry (9)
The Batt CE School, Witney

The Fat Caterpillar

In a scorching hot land there was a fat caterpillar. That fat caterpillar was very hungry. All he did was eat all day long and sleep. The next morning there was a whole load of food on the leaf that he was on. Then he fell back to sleep.

Eli Mohammed (9)
Uplands Primary School, Sandhurst

Midnight

There I was standing in the cold. Outside I heard a howl. I was trembling. I knew what to do. Then I saw a black blob running towards me. Suddenly a wet slobbery pink thing licked my face, then I realised it was the next-door neighbour's dog.

Ria Wingfield (9)
Uplands Primary School, Sandhurst

Scary Birthday

I was in my bed all alone. Suddenly the door opened and there was no one there, just a shadow on the wall. I got out of bed and looked at the door. Then I saw a sign with 'Happy Birthday'.
It was Mum with a birthday hat on!

Emma Chiles (9)
Uplands Primary School, Sandhurst

The Great War Of Upton Court

Once there was a terrible war. Ufton Court was the head command centre and ordered all of the soldiers to persuade the other army to turn to their side but they just killed them. Then they joined forces and attacked Upton Court and they had to evacuate outside.

James Purser (9)
Uplands Primary School, Sandhurst

The Closet

I stare at the closet. Every night the noise comes from there. Danger. Every night I toss and turn, sweat everywhere on me. I get delirious. *Crash!* I faint. There it's after me. What shall I do? I rush downstairs. I open the closet and …

Katie McCann (9)
Uplands Primary School, Sandhurst

The Alien Scientist

My face was sweating, something was breaking out the test tube. *Smash!* It was an alien! 'Help!' I screamed. My face grew hot. I was breathing heavily, the alien was coming closer with a bottle of burning acid! I kicked the acid onto the alien. It was close …
I awoke.

Jarrad Fry (9)
Uplands Primary School, Sandhurst

Tiny Tales Southern Fiction

Rise Of Silver Surfer

The Silver Surfer was racing through town. I was the Human Torch and I was chasing him. We suddenly zoomed into space, he had vanished. I turned around, he grabbed me by the neck.
I suddenly woke up, it was just a dream. Phew!

Callum Sanders (9)
Uplands Primary School, Sandhurst

Untitled

Gemma sat on the sofa, she hugged her old stuffed bear even tighter. The slimy, ugly, green monster opened the door to grab the girl. Gemma's living room door creaked open.
'Argh!' Gemma screamed.
'I'm home,' said Gemma's mum.
'I wish I hadn't put on that scary horror movie!'

Krista Lalli (9)
Uplands Primary School, Sandhurst

Tiny Tales Southern Fiction

The Castle

In the very, very dark castle my knees were trembling. I was really scared. I took one step then another and another and another. Then I took one more step, then *boom!* I was falling. I screamed my head off, I thought I was going to die but I'd fainted.

Adeela Bhutta (9)
Uplands Primary School, Sandhurst

The Dark

As I walk into the dark my fingers start to shake. I start to back up out of the door as I am sweating and my hands are shaking. So I open the door and back out and walk away and never think of it again.

Jodie Hughes (9)
Uplands Primary School, Sandhurst

Panic Attack

My feet trembled as the sand covered them. I was stuck. The tide was coming in. I was shaking like mad. My fear grew. I felt a tickle on my toe, it was water. I ran to dry off. My mum said, 'It's only water!' My fear of water vanished.

Lexy Ward (8)
Uplands Primary School, Sandhurst

The Swimming Pool Monster

It was bright all around, there were people laughing at me. I was being attacked, something was pulling me down, down into the deep. I felt the coldness and hardness of the sea floor. Something brushed against me. Suddenly I opened my eyes, it was my dad in the pool!

Alex Davies (9)
Uplands Primary School, Sandhurst

Only A Dream

I trampled through a dark, misty forest, *crack!* What was that? *Crack,* it was getting louder. My heart was beating two beats in a second. *Snap!* That was me on a twig, or was it?
I turned round and saw my mum above, I had woken up, at last, *phew!*

Phoebe Coleman (8)
Uplands Primary School, Sandhurst

My Experience Of Ufton Court

I was tearful away from home, doors slamming.
I missed my mum and dad.
I fell asleep. It's finally morning. It wasn't so scary.
The fire bell went. It felt like it was a real fire, it wasn't.
The day flew by, I finally went home. I was safe.

Jasmine Husband (9)
Uplands Primary School, Sandhurst

Mistake In The Bathroom!

In a dark room, water trembling at my feet, waves splashing at my cold, pale face. Then I saw a shadow, it looked like a shark. I panicked and swam as fast as I could. I looked up. I was in the bath with a floating rubber duck.

Natasha Hunt (9)
Uplands Primary School, Sandhurst

Tumbling House

My knees were shaking as I stood in my bed at Ufton Court. *Argh,* the building was shaking. Then I heard a big crash like a part of the building was falling down so I ran out of the building fast.
It was only a door shutting by the wind.

Zoe Weir (9)
Uplands Primary School, Sandhurst

The Tiny Brown Hairy Thing!

I watched as the hairy brown monster came down the stairs with its eight legs and six black tiny eyes. Mum came down the stairs almost stepping on it. I shouted, 'Mum the monster, mind out!'
But then Mum said to me, 'That's not a monster that is a spider!'

Alfie Gibbons (9)
Uplands Primary School, Sandhurst

Tub Torture

I was stuck in a dark room alone. Suddenly a giant duck approached me! I was in a lake.
'It's time to wash your hair dear.'
Oh no I was wet, covered in bubbles, stranded in a tub with a giant human-eating duck, naked.
No!

Yasmin Joseph (8)
Uplands Primary School, Sandhurst

The Alien And The Dinosaur!

One day, an alien called Pippy wanted a holiday so he went to Earth. When he arrived he had a horrid shock. There were still dinosaurs around. He heard some crying so he peeked round a door and in the corner was a baby dinosaur so he took him home.

Abby Williams (7)
Uplands Primary School, Sandhurst

When The Alien Came To School

The playground was barren when Emily arrived at school. Suddenly Emily heard a weird noise behind her. A green slimy alien burst open the glittering door of the UFO. It walked towards Emily groaning. Shockingly the alien said, 'Hello,' and went back into the sparkling UFO and whispered slowly, 'Goodbye!'

Sharmin Khan (10)
Whitelands Park Primary School, Thatcham

Tiny Tales Southern Fiction

Andy's Extraordinary Alien Adventure

'Good morning Andy!' bellowed Shaun.
'I am extremely worried about the test!' Andy moaned.
That's when Shaun had his idea. You see, Andy didn't know that Shaun was an alien from Zepzibar! Shaun would have to tell Andy, so he did.
'What, you can't be!' But they were still friends!

Katie Turner (10)
Whitelands Park Primary School, Thatcham

Back In The Beginning

Once but not twice, there were no mice, back in the beginning, dinosaurs ruled all sea and land, thinking they were grand! A meteor came (which makes me ashamed!) shooting through the sky which made the dinosaurs die! Bye-bye dinosaurs. Humans … 'Hi!'

Matthew Jackson (10)
Whitelands Park Primary School, Thatcham

Human Evolution

The man was screaming to death when suddenly the evolution was complete. He was green and evil, he even had a gun. Then he started to kill. Mickey ran up to him dodging the deadly beams, grabbing the gun and heroically killing the evolved man.
'We will evolve in time!'

Luke Stevens (9)
Whitelands Park Primary School, Thatcham

A Mad Alien Visit

The evil alien Mukaluk was soaring down to Earth in his spaceship. A young boy wanted to stop his destructive plans! He stumbled across a weird saucer, so he climbed in and suddenly rose into the air and crashed into his house, then Mukaluk was gone, it was a dream.

Holly Hobson (10)
Whitelands Park Primary School, Thatcham

The Strange Aliens

There once was a boy called Alfie, that was very mouthy, he hurt his thumb and called his mum, he saw a light, that was very bright, he saw a UFO then hurt his toe, they wanted a baby and a lady, they got it back and had a snack.

Kieran McClair (10)
Whitelands Park Primary School, Thatcham

Untitled

In the stormy mansion Katy was dripping wet. She was silent, no one was there. She walked through the creaky hall, but what? There was a shudder of light, she was terrified of it. What was that vision? Despite the light, *'Surprise!'* She forgot it was her birthday!

James Salter (10)
Whitelands Park Primary School, Thatcham

Last Word Ever

There was an alien who came to Earth, when shocking dinosaurs were around. He sat on a hairy back and said, 'Hello.' Then wandered back to planet Carmellow. There, it was boiling, he was melting gradually.
'Hello,' he said and off he went again. Hello was the last word ever.

Amy Tucker (9)
Whitelands Park Primary School, Thatcham

Disaster Strikes

The enormous playground was packed full with screaming children. It was another lunchtime! Shawn was running, playing an exciting game of tag when suddenly a *bang* came! Soon after came a terrible scream. The sirens of the ambulance became louder and louder! They were here to pick up Shawn …

Siobhan O'Brien (10)
Whitelands Park Primary School, Thatcham

A Dino Disaster

Twenty-five million years ago when the lands changed, when dinosaurs ruled Earth the monstrous T-rex and other dinosaurs charged in and out. A sudden shake rattled Earth as volcanoes roared. The dinosaurs worried. A huge rock floated over the dark sky. The enormous meteorite falling … then … crashed … everything gone.

Joshua Glanville (10)
Whitelands Park Primary School, Thatcham

A Mysterious Magic

It was dark, I was alone. A mysterious noise filled the stuffy atmosphere. I turned rigid. What was going on? An outstanding light beam brightened the midnight darkness. There was a fearful pause. It was dark, I was alone. Something tapped my stiff shoulder. I turned around, nothing was there …

Georgia Moss (10)
Whitelands Park Primary School, Thatcham

UFO Unidentified Flying Object

Suddenly the UFO went out of control and crashed with an enormous earthquake. The meteor cracked and aliens slithered out, most of them caught fire and died! The army were getting destroyed, they remembered about the fire! They got their flamethrowers out and burnt the aliens! They were all heroes!

Alexander McLean-Barr (9)
Whitelands Park Primary School, Thatcham

The Mission

Mark was in front of his PS4 when he heard a weird sound that was coming from upstairs. 'Who goes there?' cried Mark in a frightened voice. *Squeak,* it sounded like leather boots. The door opened and he went through, it was his mum cleaning his room.

Craig Macmillan (10)
Whitelands Park Primary School, Thatcham

Tiny Tales Southern Fiction

The Annoying Phone Call

This is the life, thought Jade, *relaxing.* Ring! Ring! Ring! 'O, what now? Hello, this is Jade McLaren secret agent 002749.'
'Jade, this is Peter Sag secret agent 002794, you have a mission and this one is very important, come to the agency now and we'll tell you!'

Hannah Russell (10)
Whitelands Park Primary School, Thatcham

The Noise

I heard it, it was coming closer. *Squeak!* And again *squeak!*
It was getting louder and louder when suddenly I heard a noise in the bathroom. It was a bang then a toothbrush flew out of the bathroom and hit me in the head, I then saw it, my dog.

Mark Lavender (10)
Whitelands Park Primary School, Thatcham

The Long Wait

I sat there waiting for it. I could barely hear a sound. My whole body was shaking and I started to feel quite anxious. My mouth was dripping but I couldn't help it. Suddenly I heard it. *Ping* went the microwave. I opened the microwave and found my microwave chips.

Charlotte Kavanagh (10)
Whitelands Park Primary School, Thatcham

She's Home

It was pitch-black, everything went silent. A whisper drifted around the house. A light breeze was about now. I heard a key rattling in the door, the door opened, she was in the house. Someone was coming up the stairs. 'Brad, I'm home you can stop hiding, come out.'

Bradd Clay (10)
Whitelands Park Primary School, Thatcham

The Four-Legged Monster

What's that? I heard four legs coming straight down the road, into the garden. It ran round and round and round. I heard the gate swing. Someone else had come through the gate. I got my bat, went downstairs, opened the door, it's my mum with my horse!

Annie Lawrence (10)
Whitelands Park Primary School, Thatcham

Dinosaurs

He ate, ate, ate until he got attacked by a massive horned dinosaur. They fought and fought until one was slain. Then a whole pack of them came. They destroyed everything and everyone, except one, he rose up, and destroyed all of them, when, *'Tim get out of the bath!'*

Roee Steinberg (9)
Whitelands Park Primary School, Thatcham

Escape!

It was after me. I knew I would be next and it could run faster than me but I still ran. I hid round a corner but still it knew where I was. Eventually it trapped me and there was no way out. Then it caught me.
'Tag, you're it!'

Joseph Robson (10)
Whitelands Park Primary School, Thatcham

The Monster In Loch Ness

Suddenly, my fishing rod jerked, a 50 ton monster pulling my line. I waited for the big, green, slimy body to snatch me, the razor-sharp teeth to pierce my skin … then I saw a big wave coming towards me. A mysterious monster from the depths …?
No, only a boot!

David Lovelock (10)
Whitelands Park Primary School, Thatcham

Information

We hope you have enjoyed reading this book - and that you will continue to enjoy it in the coming years.

If you like reading and writing, drop us a line or give us a call and we'll send you a free information pack. Alternatively visit our website at www.youngwriters.co.uk

Write to:
Young Writers Information,
Remus House,
Coltsfoot Drive,
Peterborough,
PE2 9JX
Tel: (01733) 890066
Email: youngwriters@forwardpress.co.uk